E Ma
c.1
P9-DCN-920
Marciano, John
Bemelmans.
Delilah /

2002.
HA
CASS COUNTY PUBLIC LIBRARY
400 E. MECHANIC
HARRISONVILLE, MO 64701

DELILAH

John Bemelmans Marciano

Viking

0 0022 0274243 9
HA
CASS COUNTY PUBLIC LIBRARY
400 E. MECHANIC
HARRISONVILLE, MO 64701

Red was lonely. He lived on a big farm all by himself. He had no one to say "Good morning" to, no one to eat breakfast with, no one to keep him company while he worked. Red's world was silent.

On a farm there's always work to be done. Red had to get up early to milk the cows and feed, water, and hay the animals. It was spring so the fields needed to be plowed. Red loved his Super-H tractor, but he got bored riding it alone all day.

The sun was high in the sky, and sweat was running down Red's cheeks. "It must be nearly noon," he thought. "I'd better get back to the house—a lamb is getting delivered today." The farm had always had cows and chickens, even donkeys, but never sheep.

A truck was at the house, waiting for Red. It had come from the Sheep Mill, a factory farm that raised sheep guaranteed to be super productive. The most expensive sheep were a year old and came fully trained in obedience, grazing, and wool production.

All Red could afford was one little unschooled lamb.

“OK, Delilah, now you go off and graze and do whatever it is lambs do,” Red said. “I have to go to work.”

After a few minutes Delilah was lonely…

"Hello there," Red said. "The first thing you need is a name. Let's see, hmm," he thought. "I know! How about Delilah?"

The lamb nodded her head yes. She thought "Delilah" sounded pretty.

"My name's Red—that's because of the color of my hair, although it's no longer there." Red lifted up his cap to show her, and Delilah licked his cheek to show Red how much she liked him. He giggled.

. . . so she ran over to Red.

"You want to help me? That'd be nice," Red said. "A lamb who works—I never heard of such a thing!"

From then on Delilah and Red were never apart.

MILKING THE COWS

WATERING THE PLANTS

WEEDING

All summer Delilah and Red worked side by side.

WATERING THE ANIMALS

GATHERING EGGS

FEEDING THE COWS

HIDE AND . . .

SKIPPING STONES

PICKING BERRIES

The long summer days also meant lots of time for Red and Delilah to play.

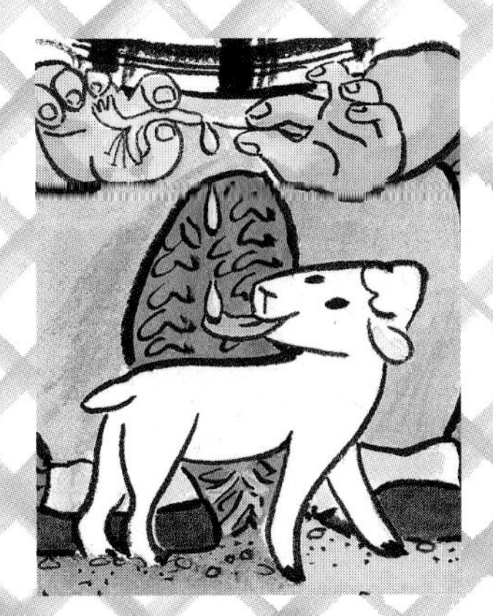

A TASTE OF HONEYSUCKLE

CHASING BUTTERFLIES

. . . GO SEEK

Delilah loved the fall even more than the summer. She loved the color and the smell of it, and she loved to play in the leaves after Red raked them into piles. But best of all were the apples. They ate apple pie, apple butter, baked apples, and apples right off the tree. Delilah picked the low ones while Red got the high ones.

When the first frost came, Delilah and Red picked the last of the vegetables. Winter soon followed, the nights turned cold, and Delilah started sleeping in the house, where it was warm and cozy. In the mornings she'd sit at the table and have breakfast with Red.

One day, Delilah discovered that there was a morning better than all others: Christmas! Delilah's favorite present was a collar and a bell. "The greatest present I ever got," Red said, "was you. For your birthday this spring, I'm going to buy another lamb. Then we'll have twice as much fun—all of us together."

Winter kept going and going, and Delilah's wool kept growing and growing. She was afraid her head was going to get lost inside her big wool coat. Finally, little jelly bean–sized buds started appearing on the trees, and birds began to sing in the mornings.

Then spring exploded! The first warm day, Red went into the toolshed to get some clippers—time for Delilah's first haircut.

Delilah felt much better as soon as Red began to shear her. A big wool coat is hot and itchy and no good in the spring. Red was being careful not to nick her with the clippers, so it took a long time.

Red and Delilah brought a trailer full of wool to market. There was so much of it and it was such good quality that Red was paid more money than he had ever seen before. "This is fantastic," Red said. "Now we have enough money to get a *dozen* new sheep!"

And so, exactly one year from the day Delilah had arrived, the delivery truck returned. This time it was full. Sheep after sheep came out, identical to each other and to Delilah. There were twelve of them, but if you closed your eyes it sounded like there was only one. Every hoof struck the same beat. "This marching must be something they learned at the factory," Delilah thought. She wondered what else she had missed.

"Hi everyone, it's so nice to meet you. My name's Delilah, and the man in the green cap is Red. We're all going to have so much fun on the farm together. Red and I work all day in the fields, and I lick his face, and he lets me sleep in the house when it's cold, and he gave me this bell." Delilah talked so fast that she ran out of breath.

The new sheep looked at each other for a moment, puzzled, and then they all started speaking at once.

"You have a name! *That's awfully strange!*"

"You lick his head? *How unsanitary!*"

"You sleep in the house? *That's for people!*"

"You work in the fields? *Why, you have no idea how to be a sheep!*"

"It shows what happens when a lamb leaves the factory untrained."

Together they all chanted,

"Sheep have one job: producing wool!"

Delilah was very disappointed—these new sheep weren't at all what she had expected. All they wanted to do was stand around and eat grass. Delilah tried, but it was boring. They wouldn't even let her talk. "Shh! No talking while you graze," they'd say whenever she began to chat.

Nevertheless, Delilah was determined to show them how much fun it was to help out Red on the farm. The problem was, every time she'd try to push them along, they'd bite her on the tail and tell her, "No working with people!" It was the same all summer.

Still, Delilah wouldn't give up. She thought, "Everyone likes to play." So she'd hide, but no one would go and seek her. These sheep didn't even want to play in the river. They wouldn't do anything they weren't trained to do at the factory.

By the end of summer, the other sheep wouldn't even talk to Delilah or let her graze with them—not while she was still friends with Red. "Stop trying to act like a person," they told her.

Red thought Delilah seemed very unhappy. “I wish I had never got those other sheep,” he said to himself. “I should have known that there could only be one Delilah.”

Delilah was indeed miserable. “Maybe they’re right,” she thought. “Maybe I am awfully strange. I guess I just never knew what it was to be a sheep.”

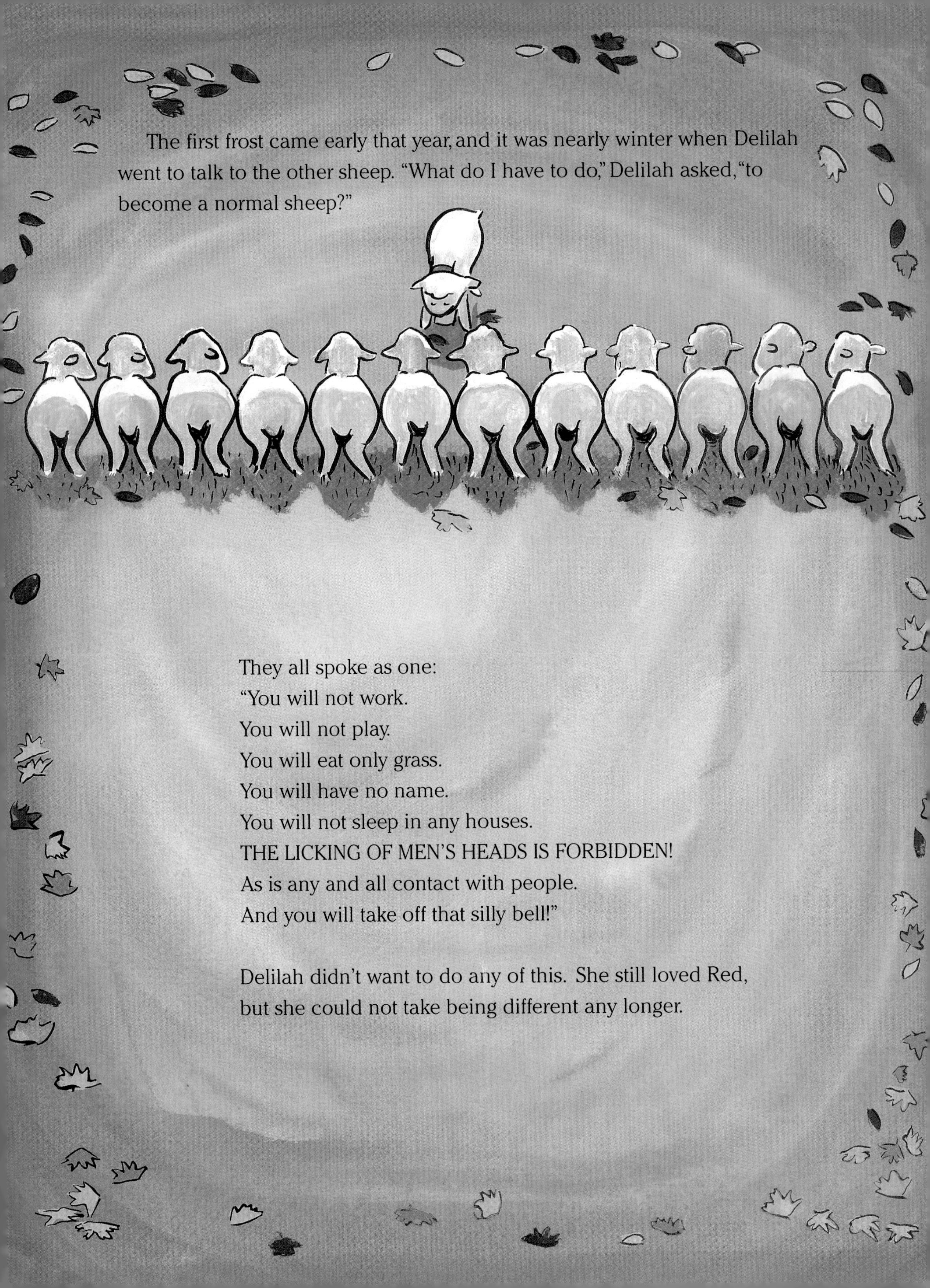

The first frost came early that year, and it was nearly winter when Delilah went to talk to the other sheep. "What do I have to do," Delilah asked, "to become a normal sheep?"

They all spoke as one:
"You will not work.
You will not play.
You will eat only grass.
You will have no name.
You will not sleep in any houses.
THE LICKING OF MEN'S HEADS IS FORBIDDEN!
As is any and all contact with people.
And you will take off that silly bell!"

Delilah didn't want to do any of this. She still loved Red, but she could not take being different any longer.

"DELILAAAAAAH!
DINNERTIME!"

Red went out looking for Delilah after she didn't come to dinner, and he got worried when he couldn't find her. He called and called, but no Delilah. All he saw were those other sheep.

It was freezing cold and nearly dark when Red found Delilah's bell. Then he understood. Instead of sweat running down his cheeks, there were tears, and Red's world fell silent again.

“Come on now,” Red said to the unsheared sheep. “You’re the last one.” Red had no idea he was talking to Delilah.

It would just take one little lick, Delilah knew, for Red to realize it was her. All winter Red had been walking around with a sad and lonely look on his face. It was how Delilah felt inside. Red was kind and fun and Delilah's best friend. And what were those sheep? They were mean and nasty and not her friends at all. Finally, Delilah just could not *resist!*

The moment she licked him, Red knew. "Delilah!" he cried.
Bahhh! went Delilah. Neither of them had ever been so happy.

Everything went back to the way it was, and that's the way it is.

"Good morning, Delilah," Red says when they sit down to breakfast. Delilah smiles. "Lot to do today."

As for the other sheep? They keep to themselves and eat their grass and can't understand why Delilah would want to do any differently. When they see her with Red, they make nasty faces, but Delilah doesn't care. It's a farm, after all, and there's work to be done.

VIKING
Published by the Penguin Group
Penguin Putnam Books for Young Readers, 345 Hudson Street, New York, New York 10014, U.S.A.

Penguin Books Ltd, Registered Offices: Harmondsworth, Middlesex, England

First published in 2002 by Viking, a division of Penguin Putnam Books for Young Readers.

1 2 3 4 5 6 7 8 9 10

Copyright © John Bemelmans Marciano, 2002
All rights reserved

LIBRARY OF CONGRESS CATALOGING-IN-PUBLICATION DATA
Marciano, John Bemelmans.
Delilah / by John Bemelmans Marciano.
p. cm.
Summary: Delilah the lamb's friendship with Farmer Red is threatened
when more sheep arrive from the Sheep Mill, a factory farm.
ISBN 0-670-03523-8
[1. Sheep—Fiction. 2. Farm life—Fiction. 3. Friendship—Fiction.
4. Individuality—Fiction.] I. Title.
PZ7.M328556 Dg 2002 [E]—dc21 2001006303

Printed in Hong Kong
Set in Cheltenham

The illustrations for this book were rendered in gouache.